JINGLE CATS

by Michael McDermott
age 9

W9-AGK-653

Tommy NELSON®

www.tommynelson.com

A Division of Thomas Nelson, Inc

www.ThomasNelson.com

Photography by Scott Thomas · Illustrations by Kristi Smith

Text © 2004 by Amy Parker

Illustrations © 2004 by Tommy Nelson®

All rights reserved. No portion of this book may be reproduced in any form without the written permission of the publisher, with the exception of brief excerpts in reviews.

Designed by Anderson Thomas Design, Inc.

Published in Nashville, Tennessee, by Tommy Nelson®, a Division of Thomas Nelson, Inc.

Extra special thanks to:
Jingle Cat—Smudge, from The Cat Shoppe
Bengal Cat—Lucky, from Susan Heard
Cringle Cat—Clyde, from Drake McLain
The Mouse—Whiskers, from Scott Thomas
Extra kitties—Billy and Annie, from Love at First Sight

ISBN 1400304695

Printed in China
04 05 06 07 SF 5 4 3 2 1

I dedicate this book to Clyde and to all the other cats I've wanted. Also to my Parents.

Dashing out of bed
And to the Christmas tree—
I find, in green and red,
A present just for me!

I shake it just a bit,
But there's no *buzz* or *pow.*

Could this
really be my gift—
The box that
says, "Meow"?

Oh, Jingle Cat, Jingle Cat
Came on Christmas Day!
Furry, little, black, and white,
My Jingle Cat to stay!

Jingle Cat, Jingle Cat,
My gift on Christmas Day!
If he only had another pal,
They could pounce and play....

Dashing out of bed
And to the Christmas tree—
My sister, sleepyhead,
Sits down next to me.

And to her great surprise,
A gift that bears her name,
She gives that box a little shake,
And the sound is just the same.

Oh, Bengal Cat, Bengal Cat
Came on Christmas Day!
Fuzzy, clumsy, tiger-striped,
Her Bengal Cat to stay!

Bengal Cat, Bengal Cat,
Her gift on Christmas Day!
If she only had another pal,
They could pounce and play. . . .

Dashing 'round the room,
Where Christmas cats abound,
We sing a Christmas tune,
And we hear a scratching sound.

We scamper to the door
And take a look outside.
Oh, no, it couldn't be one more!
But to all of our surprise . . .

Oh, Cringle Cat, Cringle Cat,
Is that you at my door?
Another cat—and boy, he's fat!
Christmas cats galore!

Jingle Cat, Bengal Cat
Came on Christmas Day,
And Cringle Cat with his tummy fat—
Now they all can pounce and play!